GODS, HEROES, AND MONSTERS

DISCOVER THE WONDERS OF THE ANCIENT GREEK MYTHS

SELENE NICOLAIDES

BARRON'S

CONTENTS

6
INTRODUCTION

8
LAND OF GODS AND HEROES

16
IN THE BEGINNING

26
THE MIGHTY GODS

48
MONSTERS AND MYTHICAL CREATURES

58
HEROES AND DEMIGODS

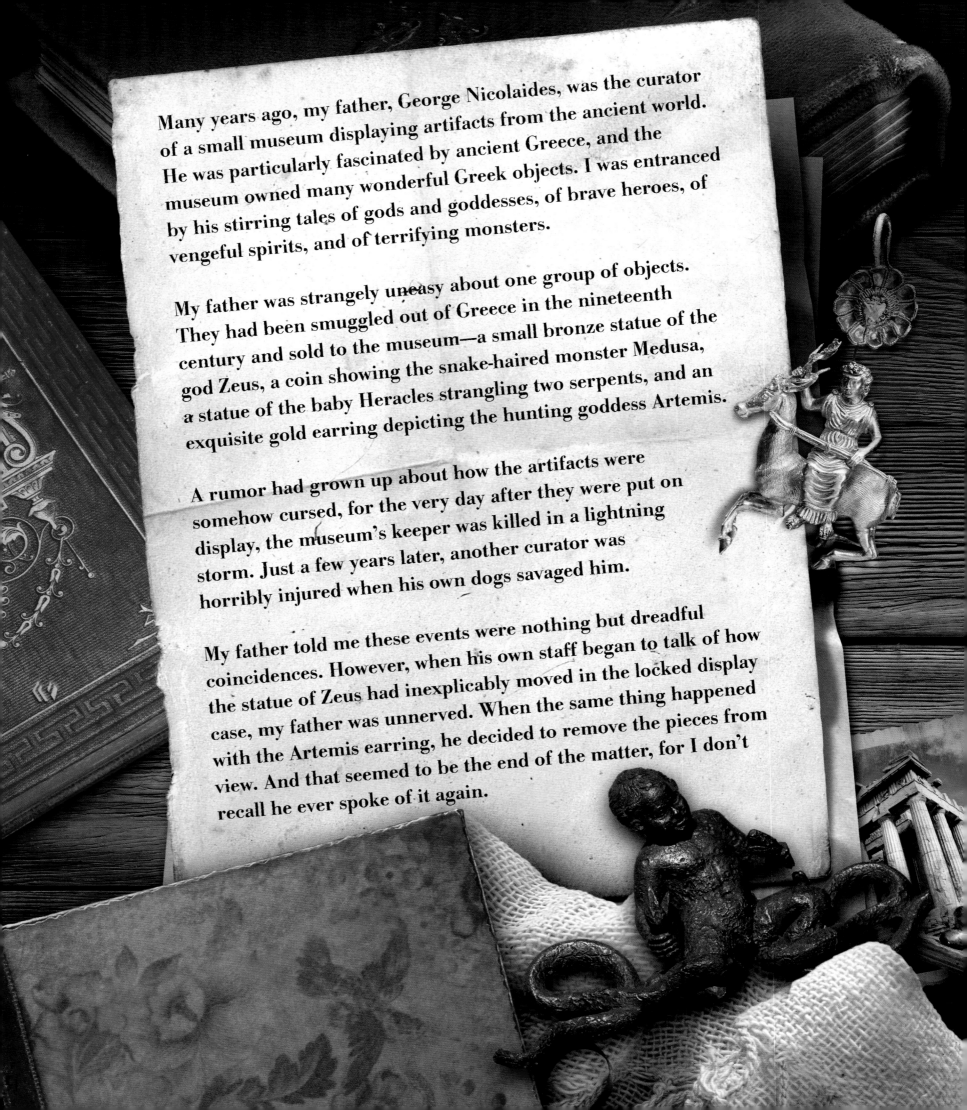

Many years ago, my father, George Nicolaides, was the curator of a small museum displaying artifacts from the ancient world. He was particularly fascinated by ancient Greece, and the museum owned many wonderful Greek objects. I was entranced by his stirring tales of gods and goddesses, of brave heroes, of vengeful spirits, and of terrifying monsters.

My father was strangely uneasy about one group of objects. They had been smuggled out of Greece in the nineteenth century and sold to the museum—a small bronze statue of the god Zeus, a coin showing the snake-haired monster Medusa, a statue of the baby Heracles strangling two serpents, and an exquisite gold earring depicting the hunting goddess Artemis.

A rumor had grown up about how the artifacts were somehow cursed, for the very day after they were put on display, the museum's keeper was killed in a lightning storm. Just a few years later, another curator was horribly injured when his own dogs savaged him.

My father told me these events were nothing but dreadful coincidences. However, when his own staff began to talk of how the statue of Zeus had inexplicably moved in the locked display case, my father was unnerved. When the same thing happened with the Artemis earring, he decided to remove the pieces from view. And that seemed to be the end of the matter, for I don't recall he ever spoke of it again.

When my father died, among his possessions was a curious box with a note attached: "Do not open—for Athens." I was intrigued and wondered if the "cursed" objects lay inside. However, as the daughter of a Greek scholar, the Pandora myth flashed across my mind. She was once given a box by the gods and told never to open it; when she did, all the troubles of the world poured out. And although I knew it was silly superstition, I hid the unopened box away in my own attic.

Just over a year ago, I began to be troubled by loud knocks and scraping noises coming from my loft. I searched but could find no explanation. Then one night there was a great storm—in between crashes of thunder, the attic noises started up and were more insistent than ever. I was quite terrified.

In the morning, I climbed up to the loft and my eyes fell upon my father's box. The sealed lid had been forced open and inside I saw—with dread—the little statue of Zeus gleaming in the half-light alongside the other pieces.

I immediately knew what I must do, and arranged for these treasures to be returned to their rightful home. Now housed in an Athens museum, they are shown in the pages of this book. I hope these mysterious objects will speak to you—as they did to me—of an ancient land rich in mystery and myth.

Selene Nicolaides,
London

Do not open— for Athens

LAND of GODS and HEROES

We owe much to the ancient Greeks, for they were wonderful scientists, artists, and thinkers. They were also incredible storytellers. Greek myths tell of powerful gods and goddesses, of mysterious spirits, and of brave heroes who conquered terrifying monsters. These ancient tales, passed from one generation to the next, are some of the greatest stories ever told and have inspired many famous works of art over the ages.

THE ANCIENT GREEKS

Thousands of years ago, the ancient Greeks developed a way of life that was to shape Western civilization. They introduced important ideas in politics, science, and philosophy, and excelled in the arts and sport. As a way of understanding the world around them, the Greeks told each other extraordinary tales of gods, heroes, and monsters. These myths live on today in ancient writings, in beautiful works of art, and in crumbling temple ruins.

An ancient Greek coin dating from the fifth century BC. It shows the goddess Athena.

The First Greeks

The Minoan civilization flourished on the island of Crete roughly between 2700 and 1500 BC. The people here lived in large settlements based around rich palaces. After the fall of the Minoans, the peoples of Mycenae dominated the Greek world until around 1200 BC. The Mycenaeans were warriors and traders, and traveled far and wide.

The Golden Age of Athens

Little is known about the period from 1100 to 800 BC, a time that is often called the Dark Ages. From the eighth century BC, independent settlements known as city-states—such as Sparta and Athens—grew up on the Greek mainland, and colonies were created overseas. By the fifth century BC, Athens had become the most important city-state, and was a magnificent center of culture and learning.

A Roman mosaic showing Alexander the Great.

The End of an Era

In 336 BC, Alexander (later called "the Great") became the ruler of the Greek kingdom Macedonia. He led a huge army to invade Persian territory and created an empire stretching all the way to India. After Alexander's death, this empire was divided up into four Greek-ruled kingdoms. By 30 BC, however, all of Greece had fallen to the rising power of the Romans.

The Parthenon, a marble temple built for Athena, still stands on a rocky hill called the Acropolis in Athens.

This magnificent gold death mask was found at Mycenae. It dates from around 1500 BC.

WARFARE

War was an everyday part of ancient Greek life, and the myths are full of battles and bloodshed. The Trojan War is the most famous war in Greek mythology. Other myths tell of a fearsome race of female warriors called the Amazons who were considered to be the equal of men in war.

A Spartan warrior's helmet.

RELIGION AND MYTHOLOGY

The ancient Greeks believed that powerful gods and goddesses ruled the world. The most important of these were the 12 Olympians who were said to inhabit a kingdom high up on Mount Olympus. However, there were many other gods, as well as demigods—children with one immortal and one mortal parent—and spirits. People worshipped the gods they found most useful. A Greek might have prayed to Zeus for rain, to Athena for success on the battlefield, or to Apollo for healing.

The ruins of the Temple of Apollo at Corinth. The temple dates from around 540 BC.

This ancient stone depicts the gods (from left): Hestia (sometimes considered an Olympian god, instead of Dionysus), Hermes, Aphrodite, Ares, Demeter, Hephaestus, Hera, Poseidon, Athena, Zeus, Artemis, and Apollo.

Tales of Gods and Mortals

Many Greek myths recount the adventures of gods and goddesses, and their dealings with humans. The gods are often shown as behaving like people—they argue, fall in love, and become jealous. Some tales recount how heroes overcome terrifying monsters, while other myths attempt to explain what lies behind the powerful forces of nature.

The table (right) lists the 12 Olympian gods. Hestia and Hades were also considered important gods.

THE OLYMPIAN GODS

The 12 Olympian gods and goddesses are often portrayed in myths and in art with various symbols that help to identify them. This table shows some of their main symbols.

ZEUS

King of the gods, god of the sky
Symbol—thunderbolt

POSEIDON

God of the sea
Symbol—trident

APOLLO

God of the sun, music, and healing
Symbol—lyre

ATHENA

Goddess of wisdom and war
Symbol—owl

DIONYSUS

God of wine and celebration
Symbol—grapes

ARTEMIS

Goddess of hunting and the moon
Symbol—bow and arrow

ARES

God of war
Symbol—armor

HERA

Queen of the gods, goddess of marriage
Symbol—diadem

DEMETER

Goddess of nature, fertility, and the harvest
Symbol—wheat sheaf

APHRODITE

Goddess of love
Symbol—dove

HERMES

Messenger of the gods
Symbol—caduceus

HEPHAESTUS

God of fire
Symbol—hammer or ax

A MAP OF MYTHICAL GREECE

The kingdoms and city-states of the ancient Greeks were located in what is still mainland Greece and its many small islands. The Greeks were seafaring people and they traded with other countries surrounding the Mediterranean—they also settled farther afield, creating Greek colonies in what is now southern Italy, in Sicily, and around the Black Sea.

The ancient Greeks called their country "Hellas." Their understanding of the world was centered around the Mediterranean and what they knew of the surrounding land. Legends grew up of strange sea creatures and of mysterious kingdoms that lay across the waters. This map shows you the major locations of the ancient Greek mythical world and places where the heroes of Greek mythology were thought to have done battle with monsters, gods, and enemy armies.

Circe

Cerberus

Scylla

Pegasus

Mt. Etna

Typhon

Charybdis

Polyphemus

MEDITERRANEAN SEA

Pan

Hydra

Jason and
the Argonauts

Centaur

BLACK SEA

MACEDONIA

Trojan
Horse

Mt. Olympus

Troy

Zeus

Iolcus

Voyages of Odysseus

Apollo

Delphi

Thebes

Chimera

Athens

Mt. Erymanthis

Corinth

Ithaca

Mycenae

Medusa

Sparta

Poseidon

Mt. Ida

CRETE

Minotaur

IN THE BEGINNING

The tales of ancient Greece go back to the dawn of time itself. In the beginning there was nothing but a vast and yawning emptiness: no Earth or moon, no day or night, and no gods or people. Yet out of this nothingness came a miracle—the appearance of the Earth and sky, the birth of the enormous Titans, and finally the creation of the mighty Olympian gods.

MOTHER EARTH

T he Greeks believed that at the beginning of time there was only a vast space called chaos. Out of this void came the Earth or Gaia, as well as Tartarus, a black pit beneath Earth. Uranus, the god of the sky, was born, followed by the sea and the mountains. Gaia married Uranus, and together they had many enormous children.

The Mighty Titans

The first of these children were the Titans, 12 immensely strong giants. Next came three Cyclopes, hideous one-eyed giants. Gaia then gave birth to three "hundred-handers," each with 50 heads and 100 hands. Horrified by these monstrous offspring, Uranus banished some of them deep within Tartarus. Gaia was heartbroken and longed to see her children again. She gave the youngest Titan, Cronus, a sickle made of adamant with which to attack his father. As Uranus's blood trickled down to Earth, the giants, the Furies, the nymphs, and Aphrodite—the goddess of love—were created.

The Birth of Venus *by Sandro Botticelli.* "Venus" *was the Roman name for the goddess Aphrodite.*

A Greek relief of Gaia.

A Roman floor mosaic showing Uranus and Gaia with some of their children.

Cronus, leader of the Titans, overthrew his father to take control of the universe.

WAR OF THE GODS AND TITANS

After defeating Uranus, Cronus became ruler of the universe. He married his sister Rhea and she gave birth to the gods Hestia, Demeter, Hera, Hades, Poseidon, and Zeus. However, like his father before him, Cronus was afraid of being overthrown by his children and so he swallowed each newborn god—all except the youngest, Zeus.

Cronus is fooled into thinking that a boulder wrapped in blankets is his newborn son, Zeus.

The Revenge of Zeus

When Zeus was born, Rhea hid the child away in a cave on Mount Ida and handed Cronus a boulder wrapped in blankets instead. The king swallowed the rock and baby Zeus was left to be raised by nymphs. His cries were so loud that they shook the mountains, but the nymphs drowned out the sounds. When Zeus was old enough, he vowed to take revenge on Cronus. Approaching him suddenly one day, Zeus punched his father in the stomach and made him vomit up the other gods one by one.

Rulers of the Universe

Powerful and stirred up with anger, the gods were led by Zeus in a terrible war against the Titans. Helped by the hundred-handers and the Cyclopes, the gods were eventually victorious and Cronus was banished from Earth for good. Zeus became god of the sky and heavens, Poseidon ruler of the sea, and Hades became lord of the dark underworld, Tartarus.

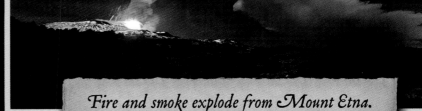

Fire and smoke explode from Mount Etna.

THE RAGE OF MOUNT ETNA

After the defeat of the Titans, Typhon, a hundred-headed dragon, rose up to challenge the mighty Zeus. However, the beast was soon defeated by the furious god and imprisoned beneath Mount Etna, a volcano on the island of Sicily. Legend has it that whenever the trapped beast writhes in rage, Mount Etna boils and spits out columns of fire.

The great battle between the Titans and the younger gods lasted for 10 years.

TYPHON

Known as the "father of all monsters," no beast was
feared more than the horrifying dragon Typhon.
This creature's numerous offspring included the
dreaded Sphinx and the gigantic Nemean Lion.

THE BIRTH OF MANKIND

Prometheus was a Titan who sided with Zeus in the great struggle against Cronus and the other Titans. Rewarded for his loyalty, he was given the task of creating mankind. Prometheus molded shapes out of mud, designing people to walk upright so they could gaze up at the stars. Athena, the goddess of wisdom, breathed life into these human forms.

Prometheus's liver is ripped from his body by a mighty eagle.

The Gift of Fire

Prometheus wanted the best for his creation and so he sneaked up Mount Olympus and stole sacred fire to give to man. Zeus was furious, for fire was for the gods alone. As a punishment, the Titan was chained to a cliff on Mount Caucasus. Every day, a great eagle appeared to peck out his liver. Prometheus's liver regrew each night, only to be ripped out again at sunrise. He endured this terrible suffering for centuries, until finally the hero Heracles set him free.

In Greek mythology, Pandora was the first woman created on Earth.

Pandora's Box

To punish man for Prometheus's disobedience, Zeus ordered the other gods to make the first woman, Pandora. She was given a box and instructed never to open it. Overcome by curiosity, Pandora eventually looked inside— and out of the box flew all the wickedness and ills of the world; only hope remained inside.

Pandora's box contained all the evils of the world.

THE MIGHTY GODS

High up on the peaks of Mount Olympus lived immortal Zeus and the other Olympian gods. Although human in form and with many flaws, these powerful gods reigned supreme over the universe. The ancient Greeks worshipped a host of lesser gods too, while numerous nymphs and spirits had great powers over nature, human life, and death.

KING OF THE GODS

Zeus was the supreme god in ancient Greece and king of the Olympians. He was also god of the sky, and shaped the weather according to his temper. Often known as "Father Zeus," he stood in judgment of both gods and mortals. Those who angered him could expect to be struck down by a thunderbolt, or condemned to a horrible punishment in Tartarus. Zeus was married to his sister Hera, who was queen of the gods.

There is a strange energy that seems to flow from this little statue of Zeus, as if the god were living still . . .

George Nicolaides, 1962

The Eagle of Zeus

Always at his side, Zeus's eagle was his messenger and companion. One myth tells of how the eagle was once a virtuous king named Periphas. When the king came to be honored as a god, Zeus was furious and would have struck him down with a thunderbolt. However, the god Apollo quickly transformed Periphas into an eagle, setting him down by the throne of Zeus. The god's other symbols were his thunderbolts—crafted for him by the Cyclopes—and his scepter.

HERA'S REVENGE

Hera was the goddess of marriage and childbirth. However, her own marriage to Zeus was far from happy, and she was often jealous of her husband's many love affairs. One myth tells of how Zeus once fell for a pretty river nymph called Io. When Hera discovered the romance, Zeus quickly transformed the nymph into a small white cow. However, Hera was not fooled and asked for the cow as a gift. Hera instructed a hundred-eyed giant to guard Io, but Zeus helped her to escape. When Hera found out, she sent a horsefly to endlessly sting and torment the cow Io as she wandered the world without rest.

29

Mount Olympus, the home of the Olympian gods.

Ruler of the Sea

S ince Poseidon was king of the oceans, she had the power to stir the sea to a fury or to calm raging waters with a glance. Seafaring was an important part of Greek life, and sailors and fishermen prayed to Poseidon for protection. However, this Olympian was seen as a vengeful god too, and he was often referred to as the "Earth-shaker." When angered, Poseidon could punish mortals by causing devastating earthquakes.

In this Roman mosaic, Poseidon is shown riding across the ocean with his wife, Amphitrite.

RIDING THE WAVES

Poseidon is often shown with his wife, Amphitrite, riding across the ocean waves in a swift chariot pulled by golden sea horses. Horses were sacred to Poseidon, and the god was sometimes called "the tamer of horses." He carried a powerful trident to raise ocean waves and also to bring up new land from beneath the sea. Although Poseidon's official home was on Mount Olympus, he spent most of his time in his watery kingdom. He and Amphitrite had a son, Triton, who was half man, half fish. Triton is often shown blowing a conch shell, with which he was able to control the wind.

This ancient Greek pitcher depicts Athena confronting Poseidon in the contest for Athens.

The Contest for Athens

Poseidon could be a spiteful god and was quick to take revenge. He and the goddess Athena both wanted control over Athens—to decide the contest, each was asked to present the city with a gift. Poseidon struck the ground with his trident and a frothy spring burst forth. At first the people were delighted, but disappointment soon followed when they realized the water was salty. Athena planted an olive tree, which granted the Athenians olives as well as oil for their lamps. When the goddess was declared the winner, the enraged Poseidon stirred up a terrible sea storm that flooded Athens.

LORD OF THE UNDERWORLD

When the gods drew lots for the division of the universe, Hades received the gloomy realm of the underworld. This god is often shown wearing the cap of invisibility, made for him by the Cyclopes, and carrying a two-pronged fork. Cerberus, a ferocious three-headed hound, guarded the entrance to Hades's dark kingdom. All dead souls were permitted to enter, but none could ever leave.

Hades and Persephone

Hades used trickery to find a queen for his underworld realm. One day, he ventured up to the world in his black chariot and came across Persephone. She was the beautiful daughter of the goddess of nature, Demeter. Hades seized her and carried her off. Demeter was full of grief, and the Earth became barren. Zeus ordered that Persephone must be returned to the land of the living, though only if she had eaten nothing during her time in the underworld. Hades tricked Persephone into eating pomegranate seeds, which meant she was bound to him forever. She could go back to the world, but only if she returned to Hades for four months of every year. During those months, Demeter mourned and the Earth was thrown into winter.

Hades seizes Persephone and carries her down to his underworld kingdom to become his queen.

LIFE AFTER DEATH

The Greeks believed that after death, the god Hermes guided souls down to a river called the Styx. Marking a boundary between the worlds of the living and the dead, the black waters were guarded by a boatman called Charon. The dead were buried with a coin called an obol in their mouth to pay Charon to row them across the river. Three judges decided the fate of each soul. Those who had lived ordinary lives—most people—were sent to the joyless plains of Asphodel. Here they lived as pale ghosts of their former selves. The heroic were sent to the lovely Elysian Fields, while the wicked received terrible punishments in the dark pit of Tartarus.

Dead souls paid Charon to ferry them across the Styx with a silver coin called an obol.

ORPHEUS AND EURYDICE

Orpheus was a wonderful musician, and it was said that even the birds and the beasts were enchanted by his beautiful music. When his beloved wife, Eurydice, died from a serpent bite, the heartbroken Orpheus vowed that he would journey down to the underworld to fetch her back.

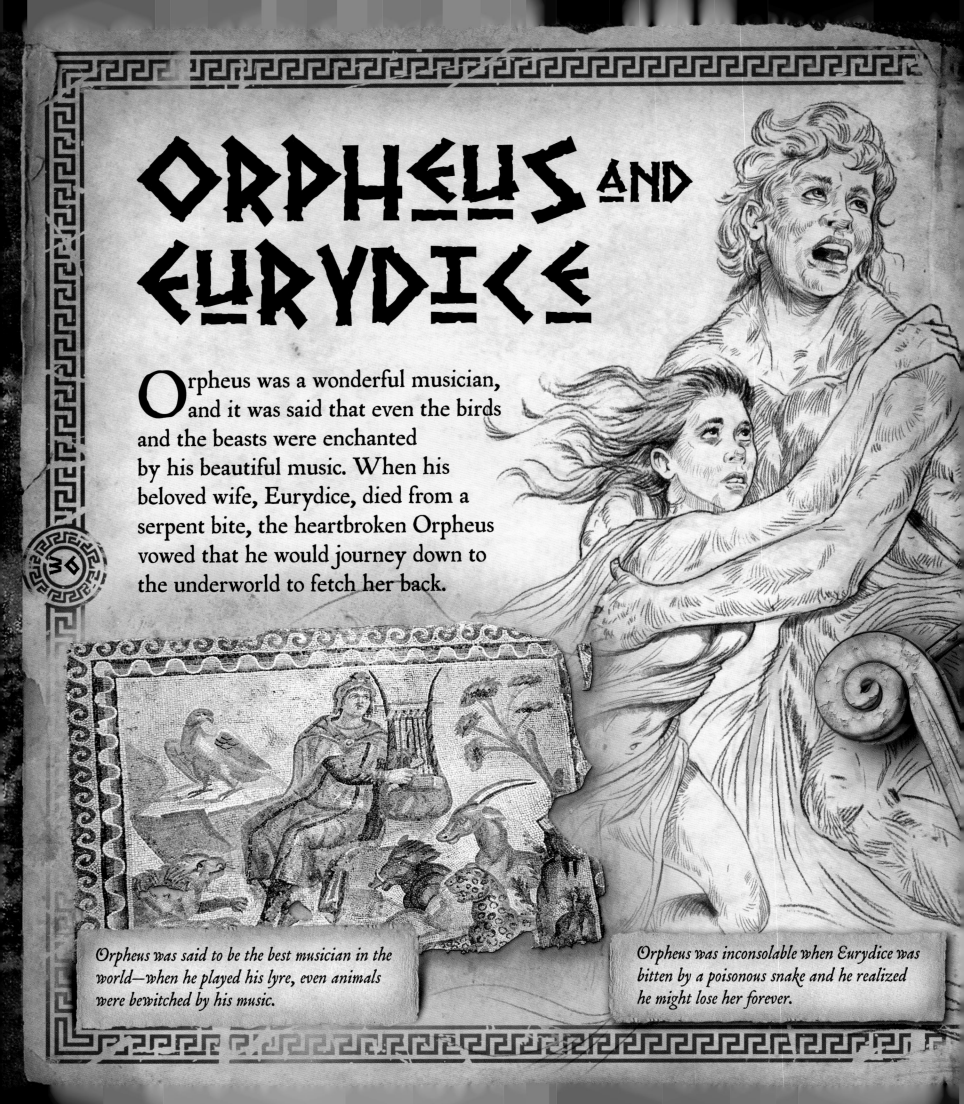

Orpheus was said to be the best musician in the world—when he played his lyre, even animals were bewitched by his music.

Orpheus was inconsolable when Eurydice was bitten by a poisonous snake and he realized he might lose her forever.

Land of the Dead

Only dead souls were permitted to cross the Styx River guarded by the grim ferryman, Charon. However, when Orpheus began to sing, Charon was moved and agreed to row the musician across the river. At the gate to the underworld stood the terrible watchdog Cerberus. As the three-headed beast savagely bared its teeth, Orpheus took out his lyre and began to play. Cerberus meekly lay down and Orpheus ventured into the deathly cold darkness. All around him, he could hear the pitiful cries and wails of the shadowy dead.

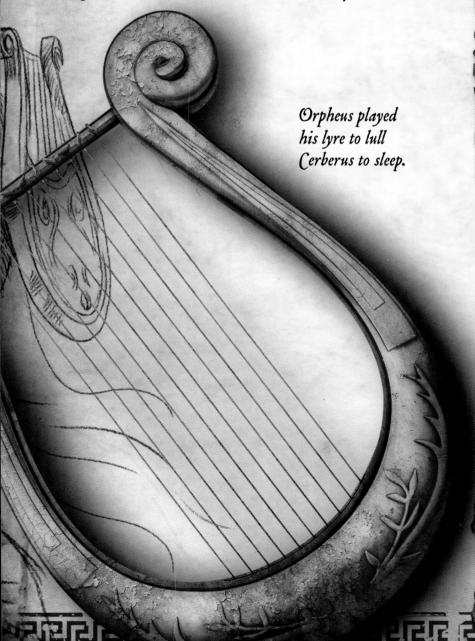

Orpheus played his lyre to lull Cerberus to sleep.

Orpheus attempts to lead Eurydice back to the land of the living.

LOVE BEYOND THE GRAVE

37

Finally, Orpheus reached the cavern where Hades sat with his queen, Persephone. As the musician spoke of his love for Eurydice, Persephone began to weep. Hades agreed that Eurydice might leave on one condition: Orpheus must walk ahead of his wife, and never once glance back until they had both left the underworld. Overjoyed, Orpheus began the lonely walk back up to light. As the hours stretched out and not a sound came from behind him, Orpheus began to fear Hades had deceived him. At last, as the darkness began to fade, the musician couldn't resist turning around to make sure his wife was there. She was, but Orpheus had broken his promise: Eurydice immediately fell away into the icy blackness and was lost to him forever.

GODS OF LOVE AND WAR

Aphrodite was the beautiful goddess of love. Her name means "born from the foam" and myths tell of how she rose up from the surging sea when Uranus's blood dripped down to Earth. Zeus feared that rivalry among the gods over beautiful Aphrodite might lead to war, so he forced her to marry the god of fire, Hephaestus. This skilled god crafted magical weapons and exquisite jewelry from rock. However, he was ugly and lame, and Aphrodite was often unfaithful to him.

The famous Greek statue of Aphrodite known as the Venus de Milo. "Venus" was the Roman name for Aphrodite.

This Greek vase shows Hephaestus riding on horseback.

ARES AND ATHENA

Ares was the unpopular, hotheaded god of war. Usually shown with a helmet and sword, he represented the violence of battle. His half sister, Athena, was goddess of war and wisdom—she was said to have sprung forth from Zeus's head fully armed. Athena was connected with military planning and victory, and it was to her that Greek soldiers prayed for success. As the goddess of wisdom, Athena was often portrayed alongside her sacred bird, the owl.

Strong but merciless, Ares represented the brutality and chaos of war.

A coin from ancient Athens. Athena's symbol, the owl, still represents wisdom today.

In contrast to her half brother Ares, Athena was associated with victory on the battlefield.

APOLLO AND ARTEMIS

Apollo was one of the most important gods of ancient Greece, and had many responsibilities. He was god of the sun, of music and healing, and of truth and prophecy. Apollo was often portrayed as a beautiful young man carrying a golden lyre or a quiver full of arrows. He was believed to speak to those seeking guidance through his oracle—a priestess called the Pythia—at his temple in Delphi.

Apollo's temple at Delphi was one of the most important sacred sites in ancient Greece.

Despite the delicate beauty of this earring depicting the hunting goddess Artemis, I cannot but think of her cruel treatment of Actaeon, and the savage manner of his death . . .

George Nicolaides, 1962

GODDESS OF THE HUNT

Apollo's twin sister was Artemis. As well as being the goddess of hunting, Artemis was also the goddess of the moon and of wild animals. She had the power to heal, but her arrows could also bring illness and death. Artemis was often depicted as a huntress. One myth tells of how a great hunter called Actaeon once glimpsed her bathing naked in a stream. She was so furious that she turned the man into a stag and he was savaged to death by his own hunting dogs.

The twin gods Apollo and Artemis were the children of Zeus and the Titan goddess Leto.

Actaeon is torn apart by his own frenzied hunting dogs.

HARVEST and HOME

Demeter was the goddess of fertility and the harvest. She was worshipped during the Eleusinian mysteries, secret celebrations held to mark the cycle of death and rebirth in nature. The mysteries celebrated the return of Demeter's daughter, Persephone, to Earth from the underworld and the start of spring. During these celebrations, Dionysus, the god of wine and celebrations, was also honored.

Household fires were kept burning in honor of Hestia.

Demeter was often shown carrying fruits and grain.

Goddess of the Fireside

Hestia's name means "hearth" or "fireside," and she reigned over the home and family. Gentle and pure, Hestia stood apart from the other quarreling Olympians, and eventually gave up her place in Olympus for Dionysus. She was worshipped in every Greek town, where an eternal flame was kept burning on her altar.

Dionysus was the last god to join the 12 Olympians.

The Pleasure-Loving God

Dionysus was the son of Zeus and a mortal woman called Semele. Associated with pleasure, he devoted his time to teaching people how to make wine. Dionysus was often shown accompanied by his party-loving followers, goat-footed satyrs, and dancing nymphs called maenads. He was unique among the Olympians in having a human parent. When Hera discovered that Zeus had been unfaithful, she tricked Semele into looking upon Zeus in his true god form. Semele perished in the blaze of fire that surrounded Zeus, though the unborn Dionysus was rescued and sewn into his father's thigh. A few months later, Zeus released the now fully grown baby on Mount Pramnos.

THE MESSENGER GOD

Hermes flew on winged sandals, carrying messages from gods to mortals and showing dead souls the way to the underworld. Quick-witted and cunning, Hermes sometimes enjoyed tricking the other gods for his own pleasure or to help humans. He carried a winged staff entwined with snakes called a caduceus.

ANCIENT CRAFTS

The ancient Greeks were skilled craftspeople who made beautiful, intricate jewelry, and pots and vases that tell us much about their way of life. Often these everyday objects depicted scenes from mythology, or were dedicated to the gods.

ABOVE: This gold ring depicts Nike, the Greek goddess of victory.

ABOVE: An earring adorned with a pair of griffin heads. These mythical beasts were part lion, part eagle.

RIGHT: A pair of female-headed Sphinxes decorate this vase dating from the 6th century BC.

BELOW: A cup decorated with an image of Dionysus, the god of wine, aboard a ship.

LEFT: This mirror shows Aphrodite accompanied by winged figures representing Eros, the god of love.

NYMPHS AND SPIRITS

I n addition to the important gods of Olympus, there were many other gods and spirits in Greek mythology. Four wind gods were linked to the changing seasons, while various gods watched over the rivers. Nymphs were beautiful female spirits associated with natural places. Oreads inhabited the mountains, while tree nymphs called dryads lived in the forests. Nereids were goddesses of the sea, and naiads tended freshwater streams and springs.

Pan was the god of wild places. He was half man, half goat.

Beautiful nymphs, such as this sea-dwelling Nereid, watched over the natural world.

Magic and Sorcery

Some female spirits were believed to have great power over the lives of mortals. Hecate was the goddess of witchcraft and could see into the future, while the beautiful sorceress Circe had the ability to transform her enemies into animals. The fates were three spirits in charge of people's destinies. Clotho, the spinner, spun the thread of life; Lachesis, the measurer, decided how long each life would last; and Atropos—"she who cannot be turned"—cut the thread of life at the moment of death.

A Turkish stone bust of Hecate, the goddess of all things magical.

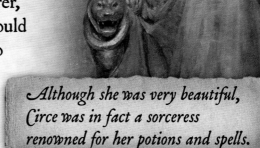

Although she was very beautiful, Circe was in fact a sorceress renowned for her potions and spells.

God of Arcadia

Pan was the goat-footed god of the wilds, and of shepherds and flocks. He was said to come from Arcadia, an ancient and beautiful wilderness. Roaming the countryside, Pan played musical pipes—now known as panpipes—and enjoyed chasing after beautiful nymphs. Pan once challenged Apollo to a musical duel. After the gods had both played their instruments, all but King Midas agreed that Apollo was the better musician. Apollo punished King Midas for his poor hearing by giving him the long ears of a donkey!

The Furies were the hideous goddessess of revenge.

SISTERS OF REVENGE

The Furies were three terrifying sisters of the underworld with hair of writhing snakes. It was their job to hunt down and punish wicked people, especially those guilty of murder. People sometimes referred to these spirits as the "kindly ones" in the hope that this might protect them from the sisters' wrath.

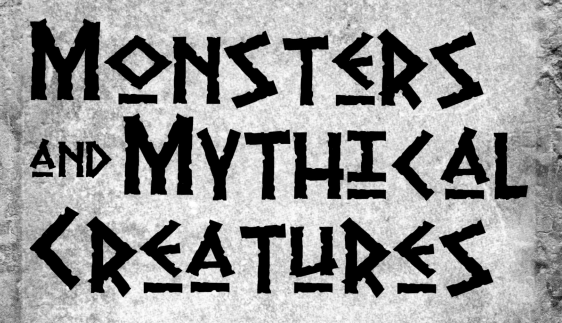

MONSTERS AND MYTHICAL CREATURES

Ancient Greece teemed with a host of fabulous beasts and terrifying monsters. Golden sea horses galloped through the waves, while fierce centaurs prowled the woods. The dark gate of the underworld was guarded by the three-headed Cerberus, Scylla lurked in a sea cave waiting to crack the bones of passing sailors, and the horrifying Sphinx devoured all those unable to answer her riddle.

Half Man, Half Beast

Greek myths were full of strange creatures that combined both animal and human features. Most, such as the forest-dwelling centaurs, seemed more beast-like than human in their behavior. Centaurs had the head, arms, and chest of a man, and a horse's body and legs. Although most were savage and unpredictable, some centaurs—like the wise Chiron—were intelligent and civilized.

Most centaurs were aggressive creatures, known for their wild behavior.

A Greek relief showing Oedipus and the Sphinx.

The Curse of Thebes

The people of Thebes were once terrorized by a dreadful beast called the Sphinx. Sent by the gods as a punishment, this monster had a lion's body, the head of a woman, the wings of a great eagle, and a serpent-headed tail. Any traveler entering Thebes had to answer the beast's riddle correctly or be devoured, and many lives were lost. However, it came to pass that a young man called Oedipus arrived in the city. When he heard the riddle, Oedipus immediately guessed the right answer. Wild with fury, the enraged Sphinx threw herself off a cliff, at last freeing Thebes from its ancient curse.

THE SPHINX'S RIDDLE

What has four legs in the morning, two legs in the afternoon, and three legs in the evening?

Answer: Man—as a baby, he crawls on all fours; as an adult, he walks upright on two legs; and as an old man, he walks with the aid of a stick.

Harpies and Sirens

The Harpies were dreadful screeching beasts with the faces of women and the bodies of vultures. Circling the skies, they swooped down from above to snatch food with their long talons. Like the Harpies, the Sirens too were half bird and half woman. With beautiful singing voices, these creatures sang bewitching songs to lure sailors to their death on jagged rocks.

The hero Odysseus encountered the Sirens on his journey back from the Trojan Wars, as shown in this third-century AD mosaic.

THE CHIMERA AND PEGASUS

T he Chimera was a fire-breathing monster that once terrorized the people of Lycia. The creature had the head and body of a fearsome lion, a goat's head arising from its back, and a deadly serpent's head at the end of its tail.

Bellerophon's Quest

At the age of just 16, the hero Bellerophon set off to explore the world. However, while visiting the court of King Proteus, the young man angered his host and Proteus sent him to see King Iobates in Lycia, along with a secret message that Bellerophon must be killed. Iobates longed to please Proteus, and so he challenged Bellerophon to slay the Chimera. The king was certain that like many others before him, the hero would be killed by the creature's scorching breath.

A fourth-century BC roof tile depicting Bellerophon riding the winged stallion Pegasus.

Slaying the Beast

That same night, the goddess Athena appeared to Bellerophon. Giving him a golden bridle, she told the hero to find the winged horse Pegasus. The following day, Bellerophon came across the beautiful stallion drinking from a forest pool. Pegasus reared and pummeled his hooves, but Bellerophon slipped the bridle over the creature's nose and mounted his back. As the pair flew over Lycia, Bellerophon saw the scorched land that lay around the Chimera's lair and had an idea. Guiding Pegasus back down to the ground, the hero found a block of lead to place on the end of his spear, and then man and horse once again took to the skies. When the Chimera emerged from its lair, Pegasus sped down toward the beast's gaping jaws and Bellerophon thrust his spear into its throat. The Chimera's fiery breath melted the lead and the creature was suffocated.

The Chimera had a serpent's head at the end of its tail.

SCYLLA AND CHARYBDIS

Mediterranean sailors were terrorized by a dreadful pair of monsters, Scylla and Charybdis, which lived on either side of a narrow sea channel between Italy and Sicily. Charybdis was said to lie hidden beneath a rock. Three times a day, she sucked in huge amounts of water before spitting it out again. This created a vast, raging whirlpool that dragged ships down beneath the waves.

A Greek bronze showing Scylla, the six-headed monster that terrorized Mediterranean waters.

Gaping Jaws

Sailors desperate to avoid the wrath of Charybdis risked sailing too close to the fearsome Scylla. Myth tells that this monster was once a beautiful water nymph loved by Poseidon. The sea god's wife, Amphitrite, became jealous and transformed the nymph into a beast with six long necks, each topped by a ferocious head. The monster's gaping mouths each contained three rows of pointed teeth. Concealed in her dark sea cave, Scylla silently lay in wait for passing ships. When one passed within reach, out shot her ravenous heads to snatch and devour victims.

In Homer's *Odyssey*, Odysseus must choose whether to confront Charybdis or Scylla.

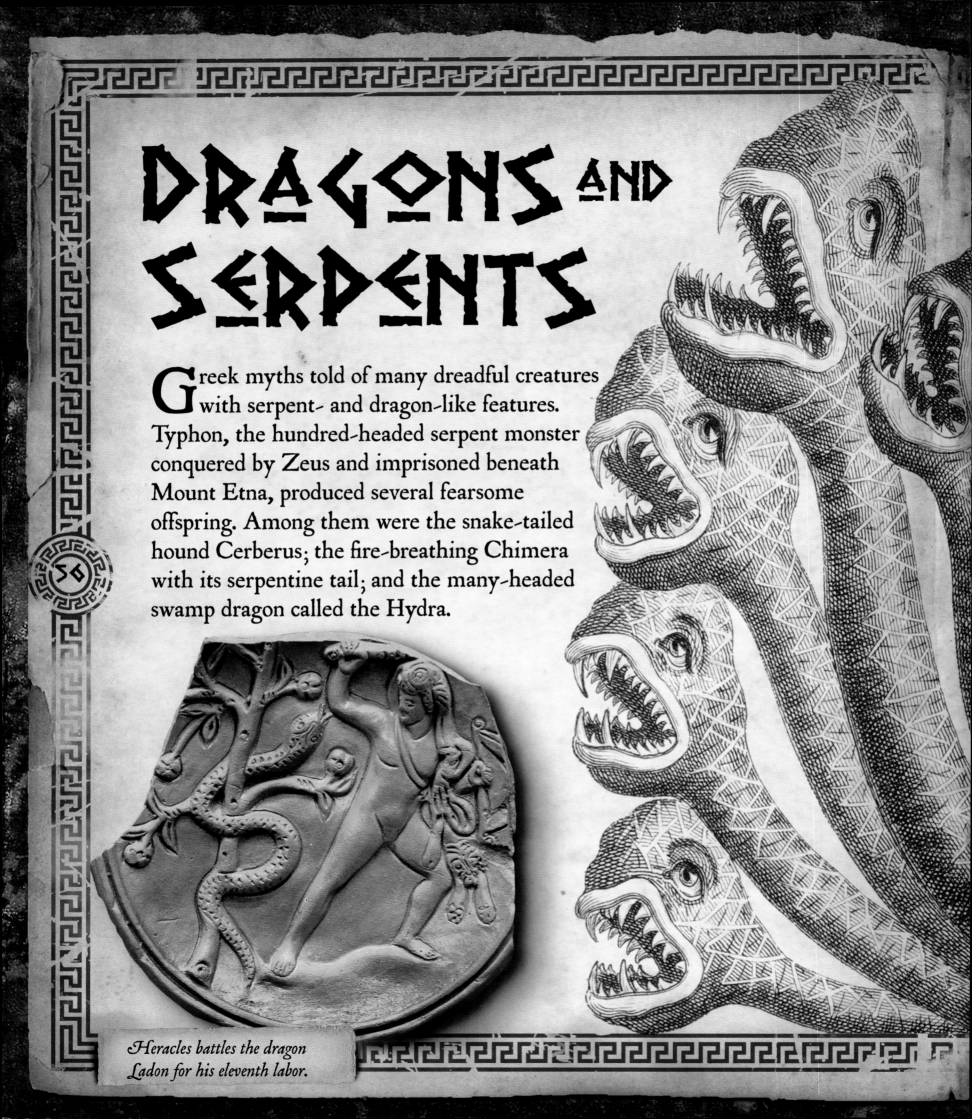

DRAGONS AND SERPENTS

Greek myths told of many dreadful creatures with serpent- and dragon-like features. Typhon, the hundred-headed serpent monster conquered by Zeus and imprisoned beneath Mount Etna, produced several fearsome offspring. Among them were the snake-tailed hound Cerberus; the fire-breathing Chimera with its serpentine tail; and the many-headed swamp dragon called the Hydra.

Heracles battles the dragon Ladon for his eleventh labor.

The serpent-like Hydra had many heads—when one was cut off, another grew in its place.

Cadmus, the founder of Thebes, slays the Ismenian dragon.

The Ismenian Dragon

Near the city of Thebes was a spring called Ismenos; it was guarded by a giant, serpent-like dragon that was sacred to the god Ares. When the hero Cadmus began building Thebes, he sent his men to fetch water from the spring. However, they were killed by the dragon's poisonous breath and Cadmus immediately set out to slay the beast. Once the monster lay dead, Athena instructed Cadmus to sow its teeth in the ground. He did as he was told, and up from the earth sprang many warriors who battled with each other until only five remained. These men helped Cadmus to complete the building of Thebes. However, Ares later took revenge for the death of the dragon, and transformed Cadmus and his wife into writhing serpents.

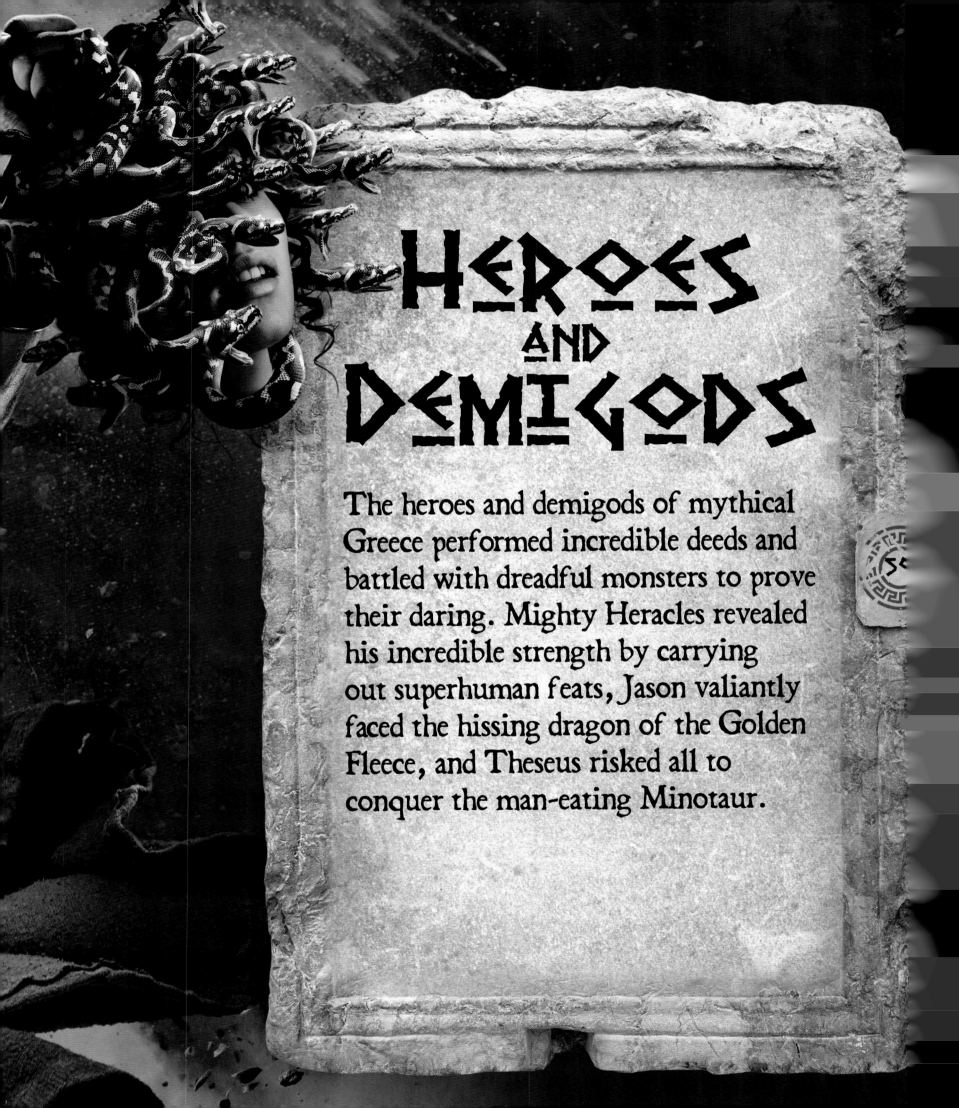

HEROES AND DEMIGODS

The heroes and demigods of mythical Greece performed incredible deeds and battled with dreadful monsters to prove their daring. Mighty Heracles revealed his incredible strength by carrying out superhuman feats, Jason valiantly faced the hissing dragon of the Golden Fleece, and Theseus risked all to conquer the man-eating Minotaur.

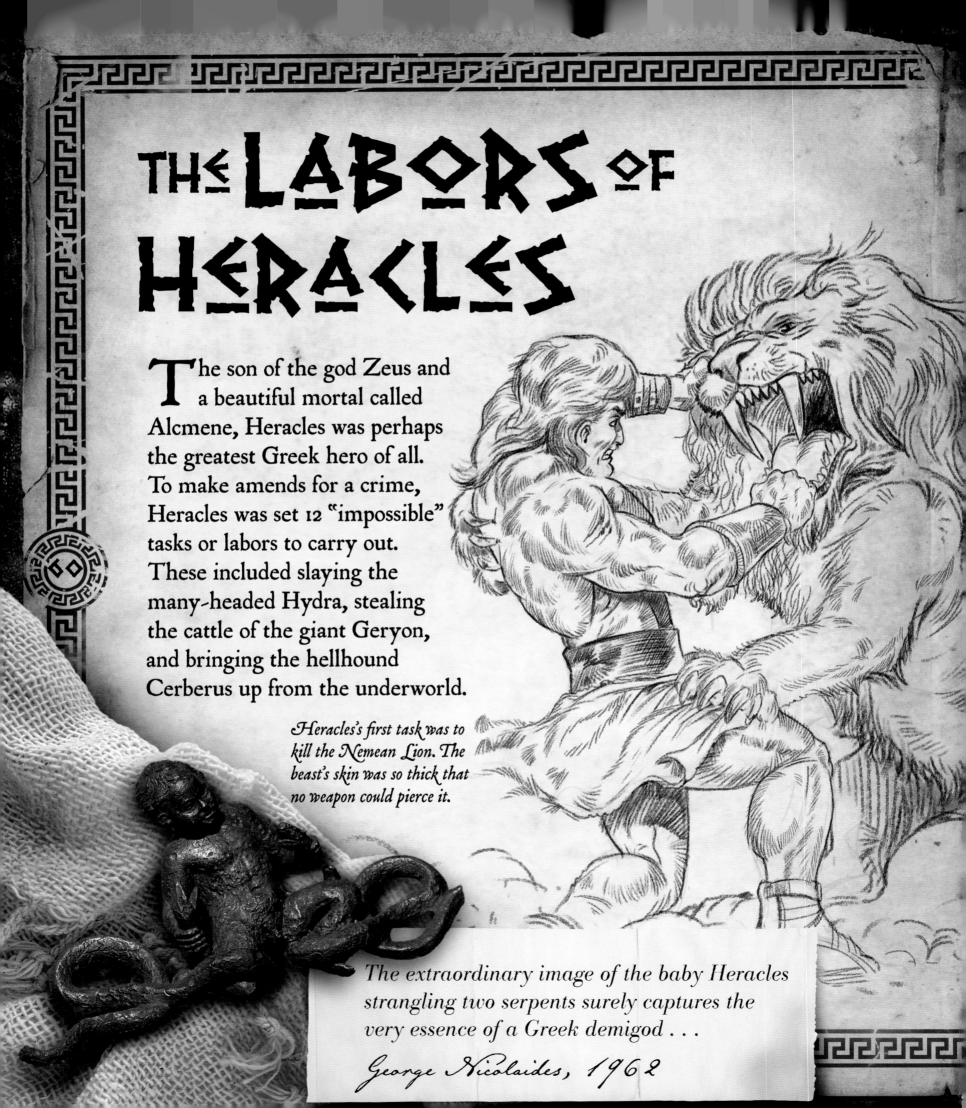

THE LABORS OF HERACLES

The son of the god Zeus and a beautiful mortal called Alcmene, Heracles was perhaps the greatest Greek hero of all. To make amends for a crime, Heracles was set 12 "impossible" tasks or labors to carry out. These included slaying the many-headed Hydra, stealing the cattle of the giant Geryon, and bringing the hellhound Cerberus up from the underworld.

Heracles's first task was to kill the Nemean Lion. The beast's skin was so thick that no weapon could pierce it.

The extraordinary image of the baby Heracles strangling two serpents surely captures the very essence of a Greek demigod . . .

George Nicolaides, 1962

THE 12 LABORS OF HERACLES

1. KILLING THE NEMEAN LION
This beast had skin so thick that no weapon could pierce it. Heracles chased the lion into its cave and strangled the creature with his bare hands.

2. SLAYING THE HYDRA
When one of this serpent's many heads was sliced off, three grew to replace it. Heracles's companion Iolaus held a flame to each wound, thus preventing the heads from growing back.

3. CAPTURING THE CERYNEIAN DEER
This golden-horned stag could run as fast as the wind. Heracles chased it for a whole year before stopping it with an arrow fired at its front legs.

4. OBTAINING THE ERYMANTHIAN BOAR
Heracles chased this ferocious boar up Mount Erymanthus, where it became trapped in deep snow.

5. CLEANING THE STABLES OF KING AUGEAS IN ONE DAY
King Augeas had not cleaned the stable where he kept countless animals for 30 years! Heracles made two holes in the stable walls and caused two nearby rivers to sweep through the mess.

6. KILLING THE STYMPHALIAN BIRDS
These winged flesh-eaters had bronze beaks and dagger-like talons. Heracles scared them from their hiding places with a magical rattle, and shot them down one by one.

7. CAPTURING THE CRETAN BULL
Heracles wrestled this raging beast, sacred to the god Poseidon, before riding it back to King Eurystheus.

8. STEALING THE MARES OF KING DIOMEDES
Heracles overpowered the grooms of these man-eating horses before driving the beasts down to his boat.

9. FETCHING THE GIRDLE OF HIPPOLYTE
Hippolyte was the queen of the fearsome Amazon warriors. Although she initially gave Heracles her magical belt, he ended up fighting a bloody battle with the Amazons.

10. STEALING THE CATTLE OF GERYON
These magical beasts were owned by a giant with three heads and three bodies. Heracles killed Geryon with a single arrow that pierced the heart of all three bodies.

11. FETCHING THE APPLES OF HESPERIDES
The golden apples were guarded by the serpent Ladon at the very edge of the world. Atlas—who had to hold up the world as a punishment—offered to fetch the apples for Heracles. However, while he was gone, Heracles had to bear the weight of the world in his place.

12. KIDNAPPING CERBERUS, GUARDIAN OF THE UNDERWORLD
This was Heracles's most dangerous task, for very few mortals had ever descended to the land of the dead. Heracles overpowered the three-headed Cerberus with brute strength.

For his third labor, Heracles chased the Ceryneian Deer for a whole year before stopping it with an arrow.

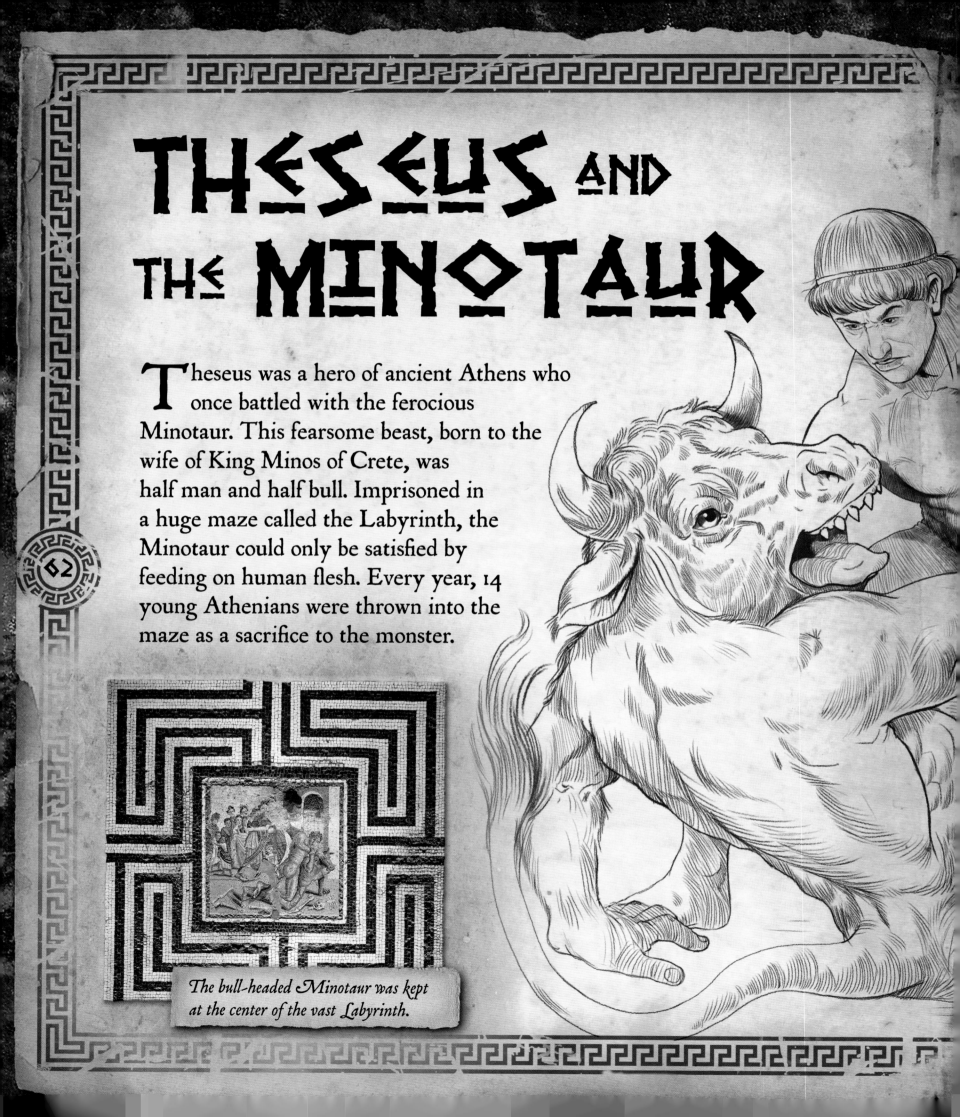

THESEUS AND THE MINOTAUR

Theseus was a hero of ancient Athens who once battled with the ferocious Minotaur. This fearsome beast, born to the wife of King Minos of Crete, was half man and half bull. Imprisoned in a huge maze called the Labyrinth, the Minotaur could only be satisfied by feeding on human flesh. Every year, 14 young Athenians were thrown into the maze as a sacrifice to the monster.

The bull-headed Minotaur was kept at the center of the vast Labyrinth.

A Fight to the Death

Determined to slay the Minotaur, Theseus volunteered to enter the Labyrinth. King Minos's daughter, Ariadne, had fallen in love with the prince and gave him a ball of golden string to help him find his way out again. As the hero wandered through the dark tunnels, he unraveled the string behind him. Soon the noise of distant bellows echoed through the gloom. Rounding a corner, the prince suddenly glimpsed two eyes that burned in the darkness, and then the snarling Minotaur was upon him. Theseus and the monster struggled for many hours until finally the bloodied hero drove his sword through the creature's heart. By following the string, Theseus was able to escape from the Labyrinth and return to Athens.

Theseus finally wrestles the ferocious Minotaur to the floor.

The goddess Athena with Theseus and the slain Minotaur.

WEAPONS OF WAR

As war played an important role in ancient Greece and its mythology, weapons were highly prized. Typically, a Greek warrior was armed with a long spear, a large, round shield, and an impressive helmet.

BELOW: These bronze spear heads date from the sixth century BC.

This beautiful gold and ivory shield, from the royal tombs of Vergina, belonged to Philip II of Macedonia.

BELOW: This sword with a gold hilt and bronze blade was found at Knossos, Crete.

67

ABOVE: A sixth-century BC Corinthian helmet with a protective nosepiece.

PERSEUS AND MEDUSA

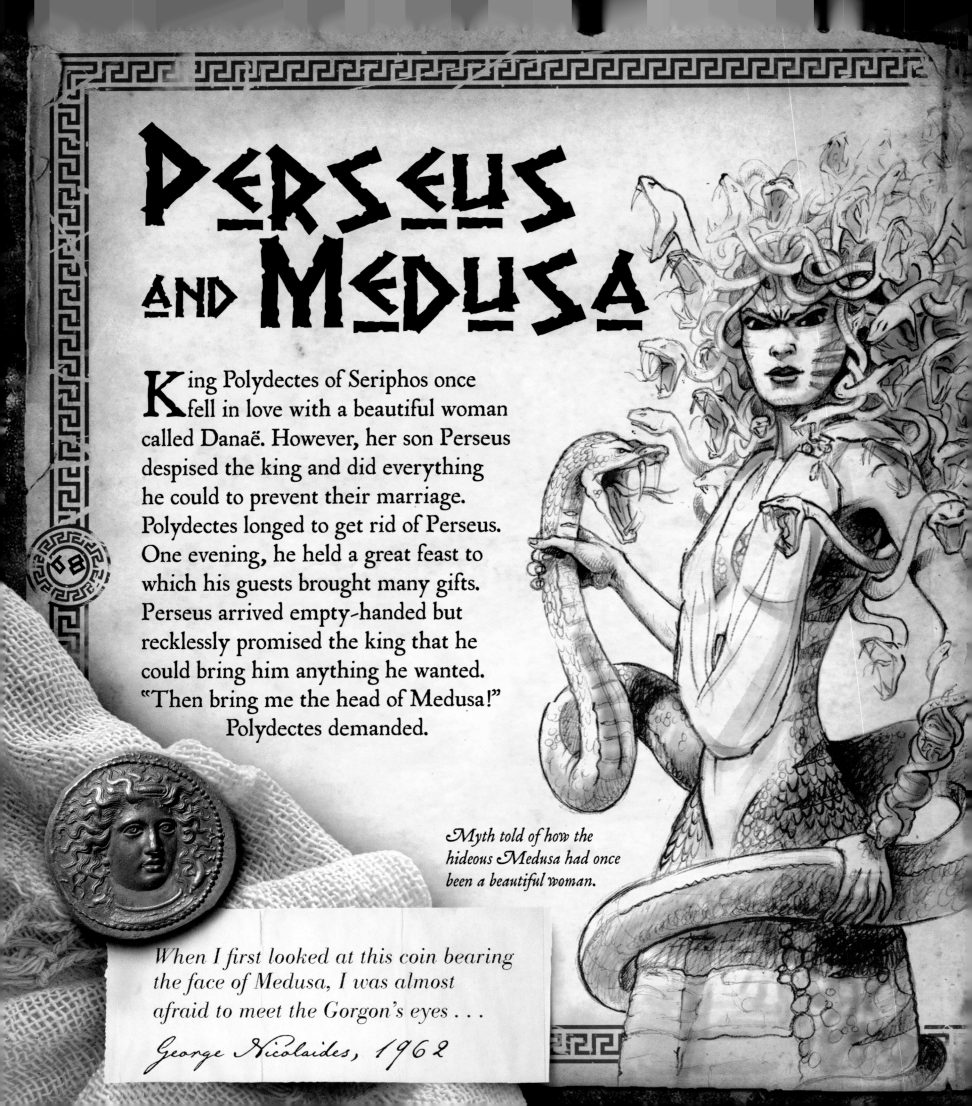

King Polydectes of Seriphos once fell in love with a beautiful woman called Danaë. However, her son Perseus despised the king and did everything he could to prevent their marriage. Polydectes longed to get rid of Perseus. One evening, he held a great feast to which his guests brought many gifts. Perseus arrived empty-handed but recklessly promised the king that he could bring him anything he wanted. "Then bring me the head of Medusa!" Polydectes demanded.

Myth told of how the hideous Medusa had once been a beautiful woman.

When I first looked at this coin bearing the face of Medusa, I was almost afraid to meet the Gorgon's eyes . . .

George Nicolaides, 1962

Medusa has been portrayed by many famous artists including Michelangelo Merisi da Caravaggio (left) and Benvenuto Cellini (right).

A Deadly Gaze

The guests laughed, for no man could kill Medusa. She was one of three deadly sisters called the Gorgons—a single glance at their hideous faces was enough to turn anyone to stone. Perseus prayed to the gods for help. Athena gave the young man a shield and instructed him to visit three ancient hags who could tell him where to find Medusa. Hermes gave him winged sandals, a sword, and a helmet that would make him invisible. Perseus flew to the Gorgons' lair—here Medusa slept, though her snaky hair writhed and hissed. As he crept closer, the Gorgon awoke and turned her deadly stare upon the intruder. Perseus avoided Medusa's gaze by looking only at her reflection on his shield. Then, swiftly drawing his sword, the hero sliced off the monster's head before speeding away.

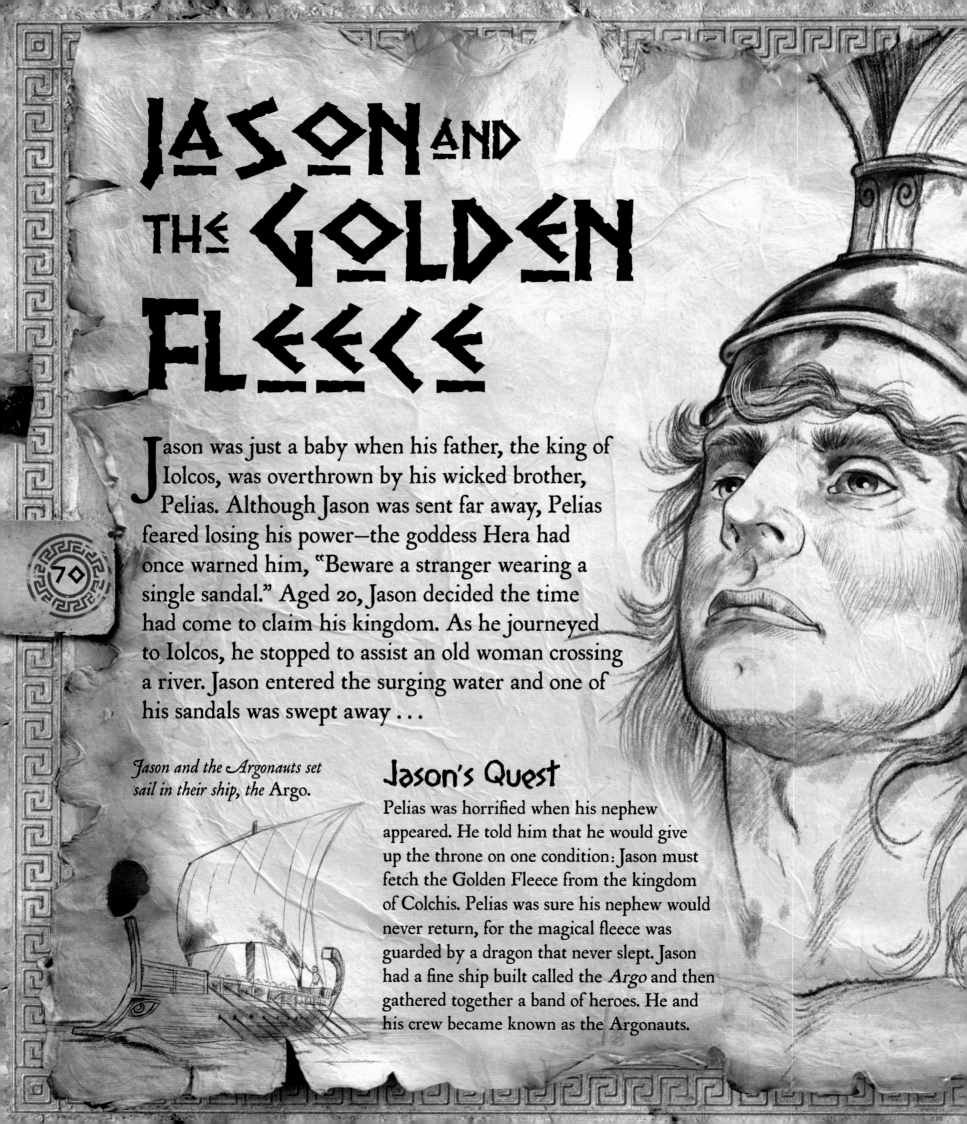

Jason and the Golden Fleece

Jason was just a baby when his father, the king of Iolcos, was overthrown by his wicked brother, Pelias. Although Jason was sent far away, Pelias feared losing his power—the goddess Hera had once warned him, "Beware a stranger wearing a single sandal." Aged 20, Jason decided the time had come to claim his kingdom. As he journeyed to Iolcos, he stopped to assist an old woman crossing a river. Jason entered the surging water and one of his sandals was swept away . . .

Jason and the Argonauts set sail in their ship, the Argo.

Jason's Quest

Pelias was horrified when his nephew appeared. He told him that he would give up the throne on one condition: Jason must fetch the Golden Fleece from the kingdom of Colchis. Pelias was sure his nephew would never return, for the magical fleece was guarded by a dragon that never slept. Jason had a fine ship built called the *Argo* and then gathered together a band of heroes. He and his crew became known as the Argonauts.

The Victorious Hero

Once the Argonauts had arrived in Colchis, Jason had to carry out two difficult tasks. The first was to yoke two fire-breathing bulls to a plow; Jason was protected from their scorching breath by a magical potion given to him by a sorceress. His second task was to sow a field with dragons' teeth and escape the armed warriors they would grow into. He did this by throwing a rock among them, causing them to turn on each other while he escaped. That night, Jason set out to claim the fleece. As he approached the tree where it was hanging, he heard the dragon's terrible hiss. The hero sprinkled a sleeping potion over the beast—as it fell into a slumber, he seized the fleece and carried it back to the *Argo*.

An enormous dragon guarded the Golden Fleece at all times.

THE MAGICAL RAM

The Golden Fleece had once belonged to a winged ram that helped the twins Phrixus and Helle to escape from their evil stepmother. As the ram flew over the sea to Colchis, Helle fell off and drowned. In Colchis, Phrixus sacrificed the ram to the gods and gave its fleece to King Aeëtes.

Phrixus and Helle are carried away by the golden ram.

THE WAR AGAINST TROY

Some of the most exciting tales are about Greece's war with the city of Troy. For many years, scholars believed they were no more than stories. Then, in 1870, the archaeologist Heinrich Schliemann discovered the site in Turkey where the ancient city of Troy had once stood. Greek myths, with their accounts of fierce combat, heroism, and treachery during the Trojan War, were probably based on many different conflicts, or perhaps on a single war around the twelfth century BC.

A scene from The Iliad, Homer's epic poem set during the Trojan War.

HELEN OF TROY

Helen—considered in Greek myths to be the most beautiful woman in the world—was the wife of Menelaus, the king of Sparta. When she was stolen away by a Trojan prince called Paris, the Greeks united to besiege the city of Troy and bring Helen back to Sparta. Tales—such as *The Iliad* by the Greek poet Homer—describe the thrilling battle exploits of warriors like the Greek hero Achilles or the Trojan hero Hektor. After 10 years, the Greeks finally tricked the Trojans into defeat.

Strong and handsome, Achilles was celebrated for his bravery in battle.

ACHILLES

When Achilles was a baby, his mother dipped him in the Styx River to make him invincible. However, his left heel was unwashed and remained vulnerable. In the Trojan War, Achilles was killed by an arrow that struck his weak heel. Today, an "Achilles' heel" describes a deadly weakness in spite of overall strength.

Helen of Troy, whose beauty was legendary, was a daughter of Zeus.

THE TROJAN HORSE

For 10 long years, the Greeks tried and failed to find a way through the mighty wall that surrounded the city of Troy. Finally, the hero Odysseus came up with a cunning plan. A giant wooden horse was built, and Odysseus and other warriors hid in its hollow belly. The Greek fleet set sail and the Trojans, believing their enemy had finally given up, dragged the strange "gift horse" into the city. That night, as the Trojans slept, the Greeks crept out of their hiding place and silently opened the city gates. The fleet returned and Greek warriors poured through the gates to conquer Troy.

THE ADVENTURES OF ODYSSEUS

After the great Trojan War, King Odysseus longed to return to his kingdom and wife, Penelope. The warrior set sail with a fleet of 12 ships, but it would be another 10 years before he finally reached Ithaca. Homer recounted the cunning hero's many extraordinary adventures in the epic poem *The Odyssey*.

Blinding the Cyclops

One of Odysseus's first trials came when he and his men explored the island of the one-eyed Cyclopes. When the ravenous men saw some cheese in a cave, they fell upon it. However, the cave belonged to the Cyclops Polyphemus—when the giant returned, he furiously devoured two men before pulling a great boulder across the entrance. That night, the imprisoned men drove a sharpened stake through the sleeping giant's eye. The following morning, the blinded Cyclops rolled away the stone to let his sheep out and felt each animal's back to check his prisoners weren't slipping out too. However, the men had tied themselves beneath the sheep's bellies and escaped.

The one-eyed Polyphemus was the son of the god Poseidon.

The Enchanted Island

Over the course of his wanderings, Odysseus landed his ship on the golden sands of Aiaia. Some of his men set about exploring—when they came upon the home of the sorceress Circe, she invited them in. One man, Eurylochus, was suspicious but the others were soon enjoying a delicious feast. As the men filled their bellies, Eurylochus was horrified to see them transform into grunting pigs. He raced back to tell Odysseus, who immediately set out to rescue his comrades. On his way, he met the messenger god Hermes, who gave him a magical plant. When Circe welcomed Odysseus with a drink, he slipped the magic herb into his goblet. When her guest didn't turn into a pig, Circe realized she had been outwitted. Odysseus put his sword to her throat and the sorceress quickly agreed to turn her captives back into humans.

The sorceress Circe greeted Odysseus with a golden goblet containing a magical potion.

THE HERO RETURNS

When Odysseus finally reached Ithaca, he discovered his house had been taken over by suitors determined to marry his wife. However, with the help of his son, Telemachus, cunning Odysseus outwitted these enemies and was at last reunited with Penelope.

Odysseus with his loyal wife, Penelope.